To one who says he doesn't like bunnies,
even though he looks like one.
—B.G.

First published in the USA in 2016 by Frances Lincoln Children's Books,
an imprint of Quarto Inc.,
276 Fifth Avenue, Suite 206, New York, NY 10001
www.franceslincoln.com

ISBN 978-1-84780-846-2

Illustrated using collage and digital
Set in Speak TF

Written by Katie Cotton
Designed by Andrew Watson

Printed in Shenzhen, Guangdong, China

1 3 5 7 9 8 6 4 2

DEAR BUNNY...

Written by
Katie Cotton

Illustrated by
Blanca Gómez

Frances Lincoln
Children's Books

Dear Bunny,
Today you asked me, "What's your favorite thing in the world?"
I like so many things, I decided to write them all down.

I like the mornings, when you wake me up
and help me find my shoes and socks.
You always know which ones are my favorites.

I like breakfast, and so do you!
I think oatmeal is the yummiest
but you like toast and jam.

You always blow on my oatmeal so it's not too hot.
That's because you are a very nice bunny.

When we've finished eating,
I like going on the swings.
You never mind that I can
go higher than you.

I will push you and
then you can go high too!

I like when we play together,
kicking leaves, and throwing balls,
and climbing trees!
It's so much fun to play . . .

But sometimes, I like it when we sit and watch.

I like going to the zoo lots and lots!
But sometimes I get scared of the chimpanzee.

You are the bravest bunny I know,
and when you hold my hand, I feel braver, too.

I like the end of the day,
because then it's bathtime.
We always play splashing!
I always like it, too.

But sometimes I can splash too hard
and then I have to say sorry.

I like laughing with you lots . . .

But I like that you're there when I'm sad too.

I think maybe my favorite thing
is when we look at the stars.
Someday we will count them all!

Or maybe my favorite thing is story time.
I like your stories. They are very good
and they give me good dreams.

Dear Bunny,

I've decided I like all the things we do together . . .

But my favorite thing in the world is YOU!